First Day Jitters

WHISPERING COYOTE

A Charlesbridge Imprint

SH

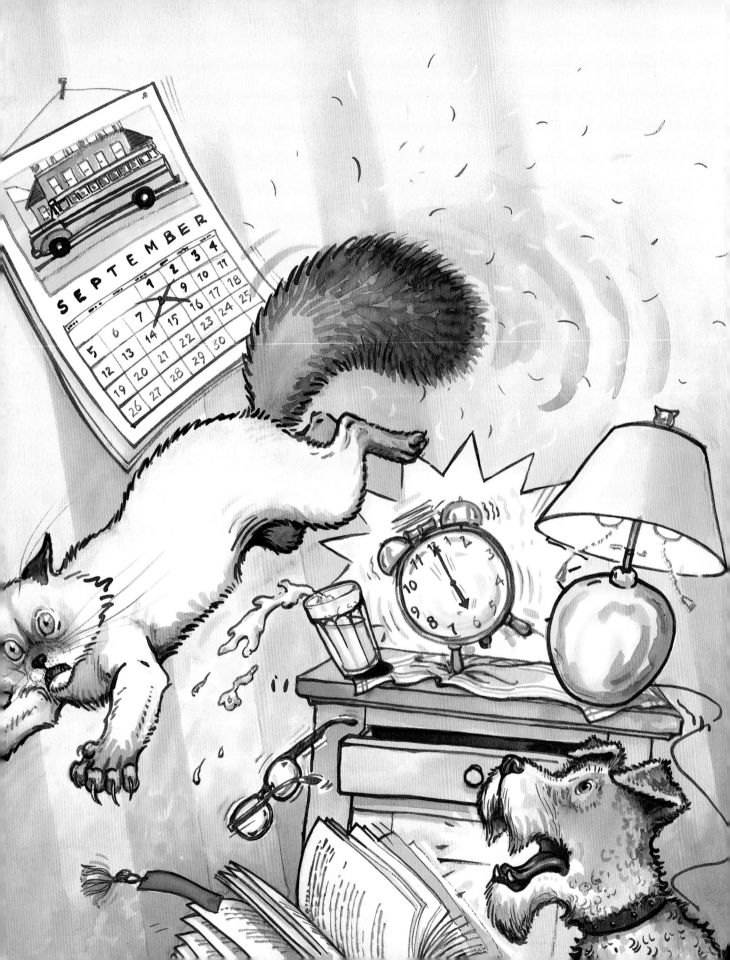

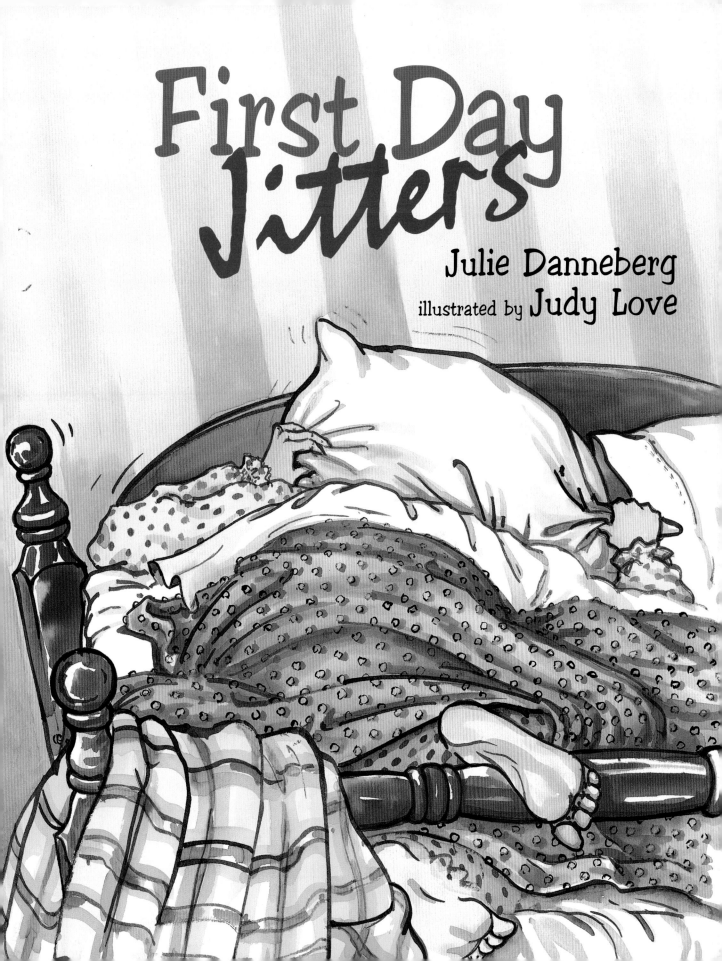

To Jack and Buddie
·J.D.

For Matthew, who never gets "first day jitters,"
but willingly posed for me anyway, with love
·J.L.

Text copyright © 2000 by Julie Danneberg
Illustrations copyright © 2000 by Judy Love
All rights reserved, including the right of reproduction
in whole or in part in any form.

A *Whispering Coyote Book*
Published by Charlesbridge Publishing
85 Main Street
Watertown, MA 02472
(617) 926-0329
www.charlesbridge.com

Printed in China
(hc) 10 9 8 7 6 5 4 3
(sc) 10 9 8 7 6 5 4
The illustrations in this book were done in ink and watercolors
on 100% Rag Strathmore Bristol Vellum.
The display type and text type were set in Disney Print, Mistral, and Electra.
Separated and manufactured by Regent Publishing Services
Book production and design by *The Kids at Our House*

CIP available upon request

ISBN 1-58089-054-7 (reinforced for library use)
ISBN 1-58089-061-X (softcover)

"Sarah, dear, time to get out of bed," Mr. Hartwell said, poking his head through the bedroom doorway. "You don't want to miss the first day at your new school do you?"

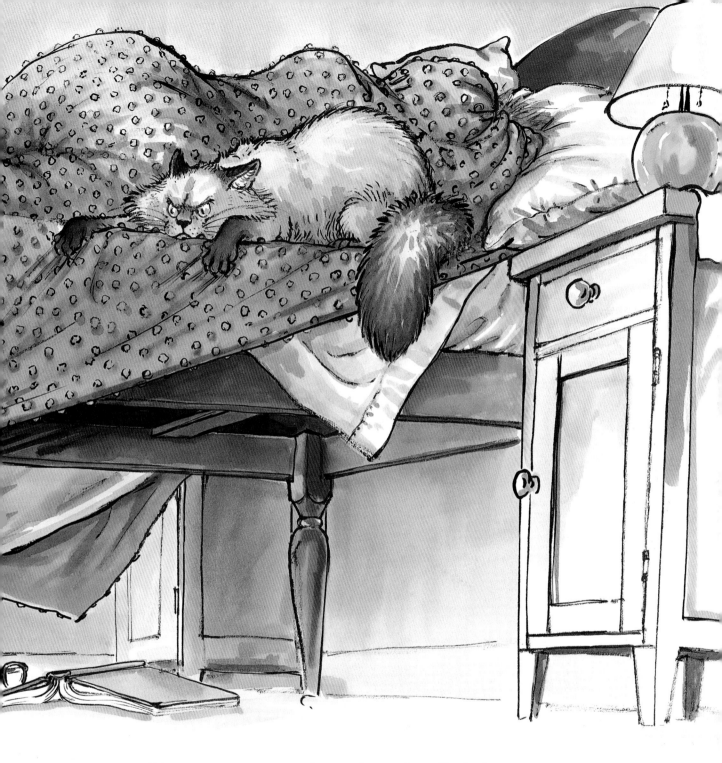

"I'm not going," said Sarah, and pulled the covers over her head.

"Of course you're going, honey," said Mr. Hartwell, as he walked over to the window and snapped up the shade.

"No, I'm not. I don't want to start over again. I hate my new school," Sarah said. She tunneled down to the end of her bed.

"How can you hate your new school, sweetheart?"
Mr. Hartwell chuckled. "You've never been there
before! Don't worry. You liked your other school,
you'll like this one. Besides, just think of all the new
friends you'll meet."

"That's just it. I don't know anybody, and it will be hard, and...I just hate it, that's all."

"What will everyone think if you aren't there?
We told them you were coming!"

"They will think that I am lucky and they will wish that they were at home in bed like me."

Mr. Hartwell sighed. "Sarah Jane Hartwell, I'm not playing this silly game one second longer. I'll see you downstairs in five minutes."

Sarah tumbled out of bed.

She stumbled into the bathroom.

She fumbled into her clothes.

"My head hurts," she moaned as she trudged into the kitchen.

Mr. Hartwell handed Sarah a piece of toast and her lunchbox.

They walked to the car. Sarah's
hands were cold and clammy.

They drove down the street.
She couldn't breathe.

And then they were there.
"I feel sick," said Sarah weakly.

"Nonsense," said Mr. Hartwell. "You'll love your new school once you get started. Oh, look. There's your principal, Mrs. Burton."

Sarah slumped down in her seat.

"Oh, Sarah," Mrs. Burton gushed, peeking into the car. "There you are. Come on. I'll show you where to go."

She led Sarah into the building and walked quickly through the crowded hallways. "Don't worry. Everyone is nervous the first day," she said over her shoulder as Sarah rushed to keep up.

When they got to
the classroom, most of
the children were
already in their seats.

The class looked up as Mrs. Burton cleared her throat.

"Class. Class. Attention, please," said Mrs. Burton.

When the class was quiet she led Sarah to the front of the room and said, "Class, I would like you to meet...

...your new teacher, Mrs. Sarah Jane Hartwell."